MY RHINO IS BETTER THAN YOURS!

MY RHINO IS BETTER THAN YOURS!
is a DAVID FICKLING BOOK
First published in Great Britain in 2020 by David Fickling Books,
31 Beaumont Street, Oxford, OX1 2NP
978-1-78845-075-1   www.davidficklingbooks.com
Text and illustrations © Bec Barnes, 2020

1 3 5 7 9 10 8 6 4 2

WARNING: MY RHINO IS BETTER THAN YOURS!

Papers used by David Fickling Books are from responsible sources.
DAVID FICKLING BOOKS Reg. No. 8340307
A CIP catalogue record for this book is available from the British Library.

Printed and bound in China by Toppan Leefung
Edited by Alice Corrie & designed by Ness Wood

BEC BARNES

David Fickling Books

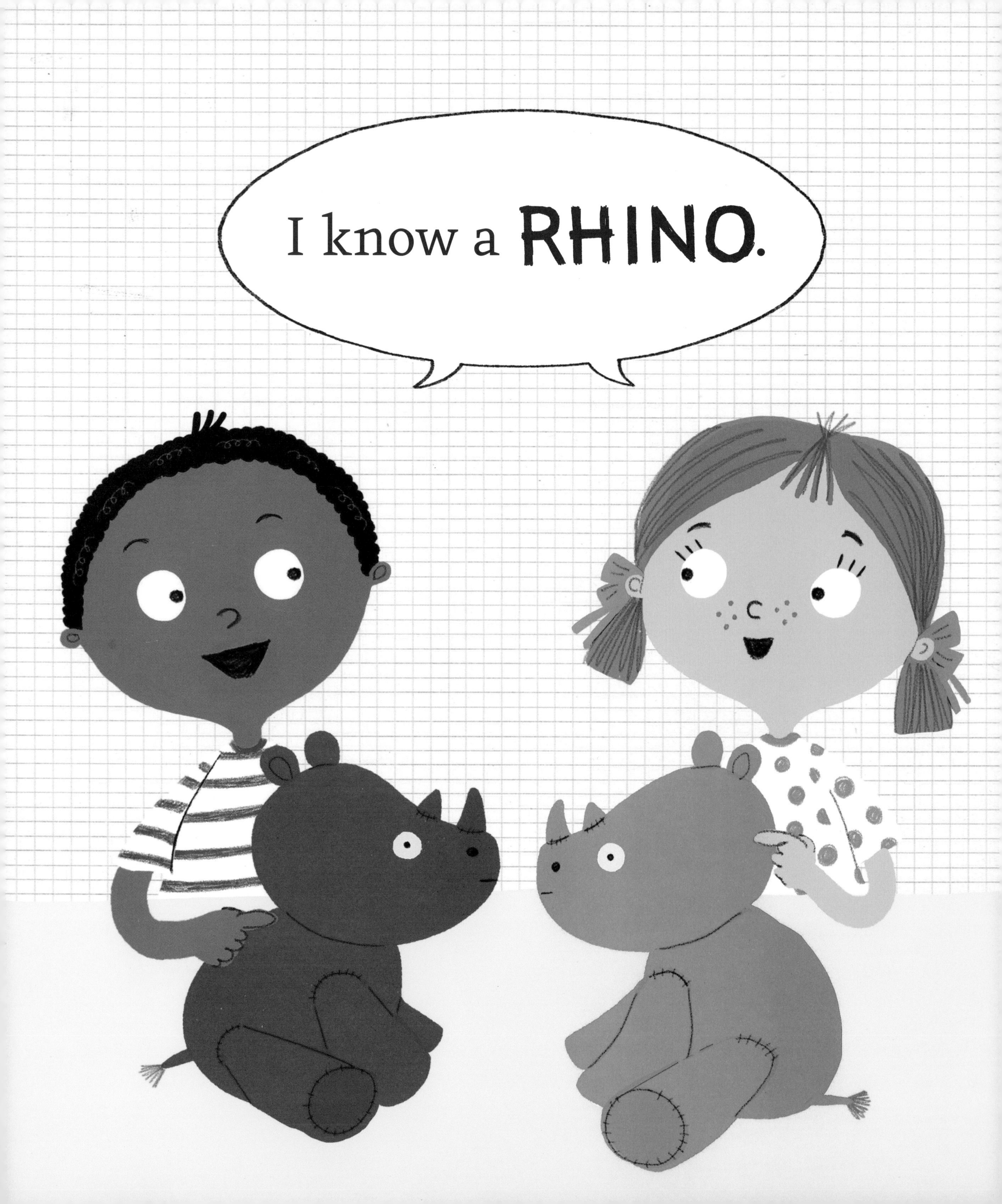
I know a RHINO.

The **RHINO** that I know
Is **MIGHTY** and **STRONG**.

She can carry two hippos
Then run all day long!

Well, the **RHINO** that I know
Is *DARING* and *BRAVE.*

He is first on the scene
When there's someone to save.

The **RHINO** that I know
Is friends with the bugs.

She shrinks really tiny
To give them all hugs!

The **RHINO** that I know

Grows as **BIG** as can be

With his head in the clouds

And his feet in the sea!

The RHINO that I Know

is BETTER than yours!

The **RHINO** that I know
Has incredible talents.
There isn't a thing
She can't **juggle**
or **balance!**

She can **swing**
upside down
From a flying trapeze.

Make giraffes **disappear,** Leaving only their knees!

She can *twirl* on a tightrope

While her fans all applaud her . . .

She won

RHINO'S GOT TALENT

All the judges ADORED her!

The **RHINO** that I know

Is *Stylish* and *chic*.

He wears **FABULOUS** outfits

Each day of the week.

On Sunday a **sari**,

On Monday in **LEATHERS**,

On Tuesday all *knitted*,

And on Wednesday, just *Feathers!*

On Thursday a **wetsuit**,

On Friday in **armour**,

And on Saturday

he likes to dress up as a . . .

The RHINO that I Know

is BETTER than yours!

The **RHINO** that YOU know

Has a **BIG smelly** bottom!

We need pegs on our noses . . .

Oh no!
We forgot 'em!

But the **RHINO** that I know
Smells of flowers in spring!

Her bottom perfume
Makes the nightingales **Sing**!

The **RHINO** that YOU know
Is **INCREDIBLY RUDE**,

She talks with her mouth *full*
And **plays** with her food!

The **RHINO** that I know
Takes his afternoon teas
With *dainties* and *fancies*

And **ALWAYS** says **PLEASE.**

Well, the RHINO
that I know
Can fly to the
STARS!

And the RHINO that I know
Is ALREADY on MARS!

HANG ON!
WHAT'S THAT
NOISE?

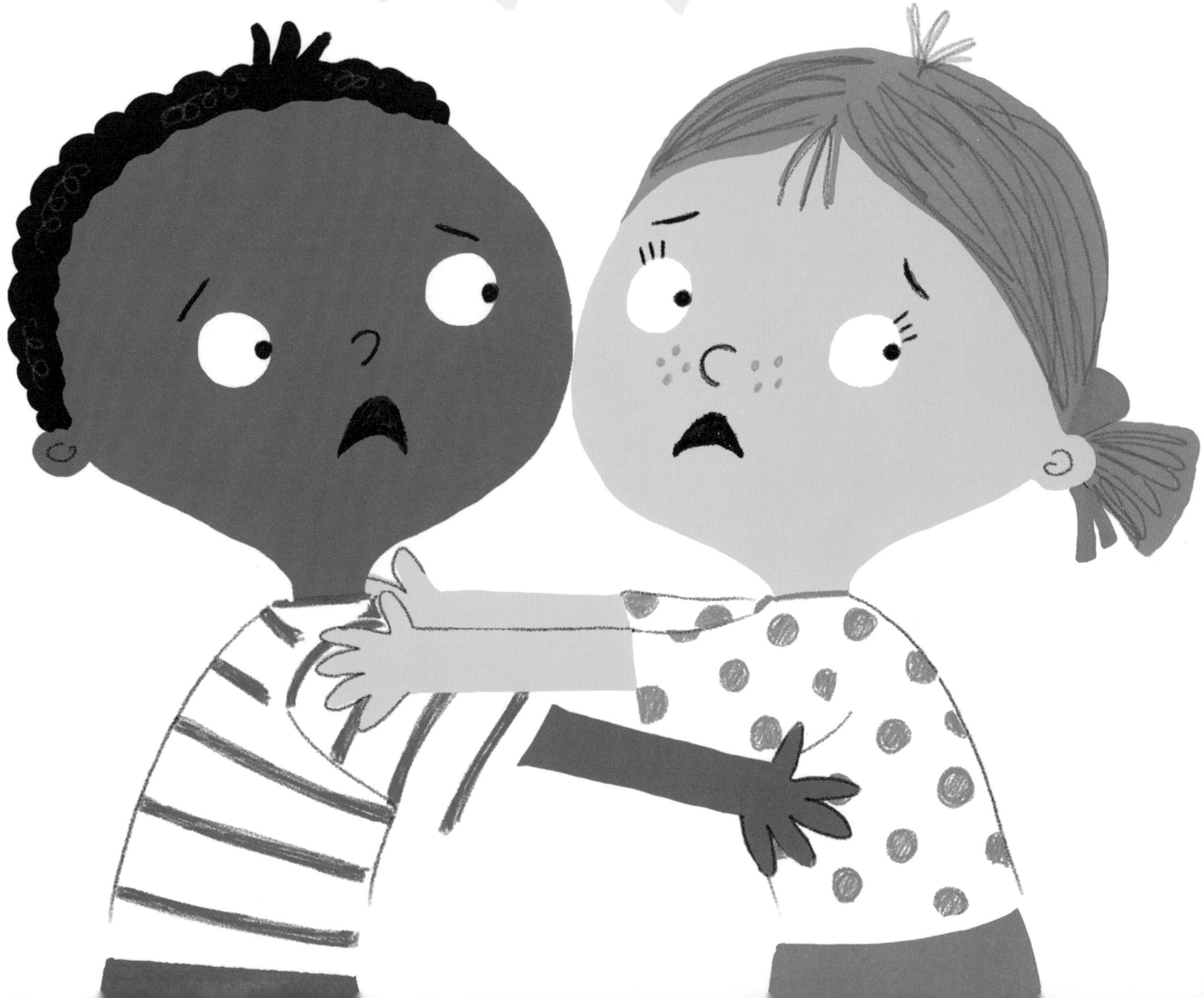

A "rumbly" THUMP
With a **Snort** and a QUAKING,
A **GRUMBLY GRUNT**
And the ground's started

SHAKING!

A **RHINO** THAT'S **REAL!**
A **REALLY REAL**
RHINO!

That's definitely **NOT**
The **RHINO** that I know!

RUUUUN!

RUUUUN!

Well, the CHILDREN
that I know
Are tasty and
YUMMY!*
The rumbling you heard
Was my
BIG EMPTY
TUMMY!

*Rhinos don't really eat children – they're plant-eaters!